Mythical Creatures
MERMAIDS

BY LISA OWINGS

BELLWETHER MEDIA • MINNEAPOLIS, MN

Torque brims with excitement perfect for thrill-seekers of all kinds. Discover daring survival skills, explore uncharted worlds, and marvel at mighty engines and extreme sports. In *Torque* books, anything can happen. Are you ready?

This edition first published in 2021 by Bellwether Media, Inc.

No part of this publication may be reproduced in whole or in part without written permission of the publisher.
For information regarding permission, write to Bellwether Media, Inc., Attention: Permissions Department,
6012 Blue Circle Drive, Minnetonka, MN 55343.

Library of Congress Cataloging-in-Publication Data

Names: Owings, Lisa, author.
Title: Mermaids / by Lisa Owings.
Description: Minneapolis, MN : Bellwether Media, 2021. | Series: Mythical creatures | Includes bibliographical references and index. | Audience: Ages 7-12 | Audience: Grades 4-6 | Summary: "Engaging images accompany information about mermaids. The combination of high-interest subject matter and light text is intended for students in grades 3 through 7"-Provided by publisher.
Identifiers: LCCN 2020014938 (print) | LCCN 2020014939 (ebook) | ISBN 9781644872758 | ISBN 9781681037387 (ebook)
Subjects: LCSH: Mermaids–Juvenile literature.
Classification: LCC GR910 .O95 2021 (print) | LCC GR910 (ebook) | DDC 398/.45–dc23
LC record available at https://lccn.loc.gov/2020014938
LC ebook record available at https://lccn.loc.gov/2020014939

Text copyright © 2021 by Bellwether Media, Inc. TORQUE and associated logos are trademarks and/or registered trademarks of Bellwether Media, Inc.

Editor: Rebecca Sabelko   Designer: Josh Brink

Printed in the United States of America, North Mankato, MN.

TABLE OF CONTENTS

A BAD OMEN	4
WATER GODS, SIRENS, AND SIGHTINGS	10
THE NOT-SO-SCARY MERMAID	18
GLOSSARY	22
TO LEARN MORE	23
INDEX	24

A BAD OMEN

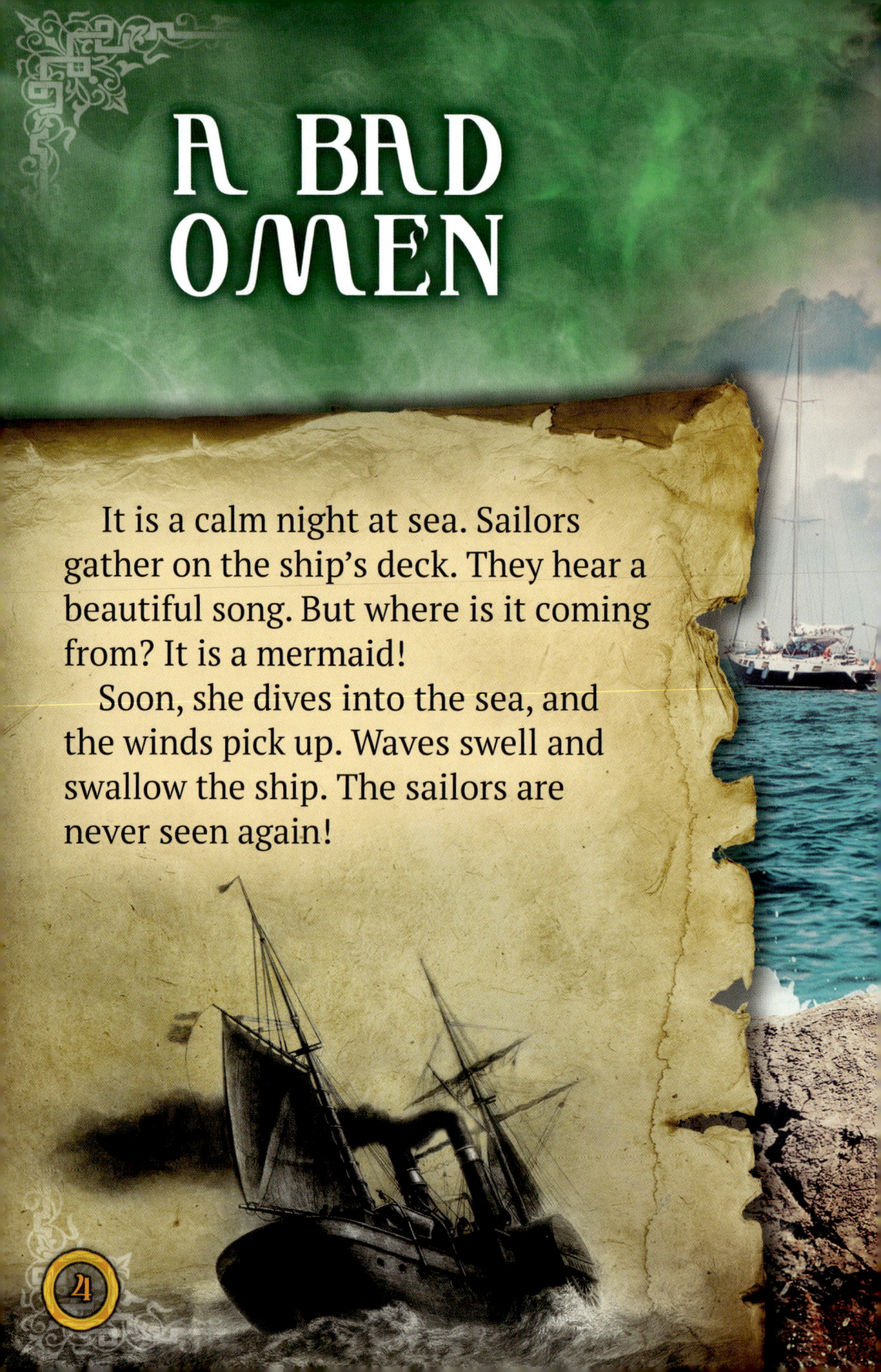

It is a calm night at sea. Sailors gather on the ship's deck. They hear a beautiful song. But where is it coming from? It is a mermaid!

Soon, she dives into the sea, and the winds pick up. Waves swell and swallow the ship. The sailors are never seen again!

Mermaids are mythical creatures found in stories across the world. They look like women from the waist up. But scaly fish tails make up their lower bodies.

Mermaids are said to live in the sea. In stories, they are often seen sitting on rocks. Sometimes they comb their long hair while gazing into a mirror. Mermaids love to sing and are known for their beautiful voices.

Mermen

Some tales describe mermaids who live with mermen under the sea. Mermen are said to be more private. They are rarely seen.

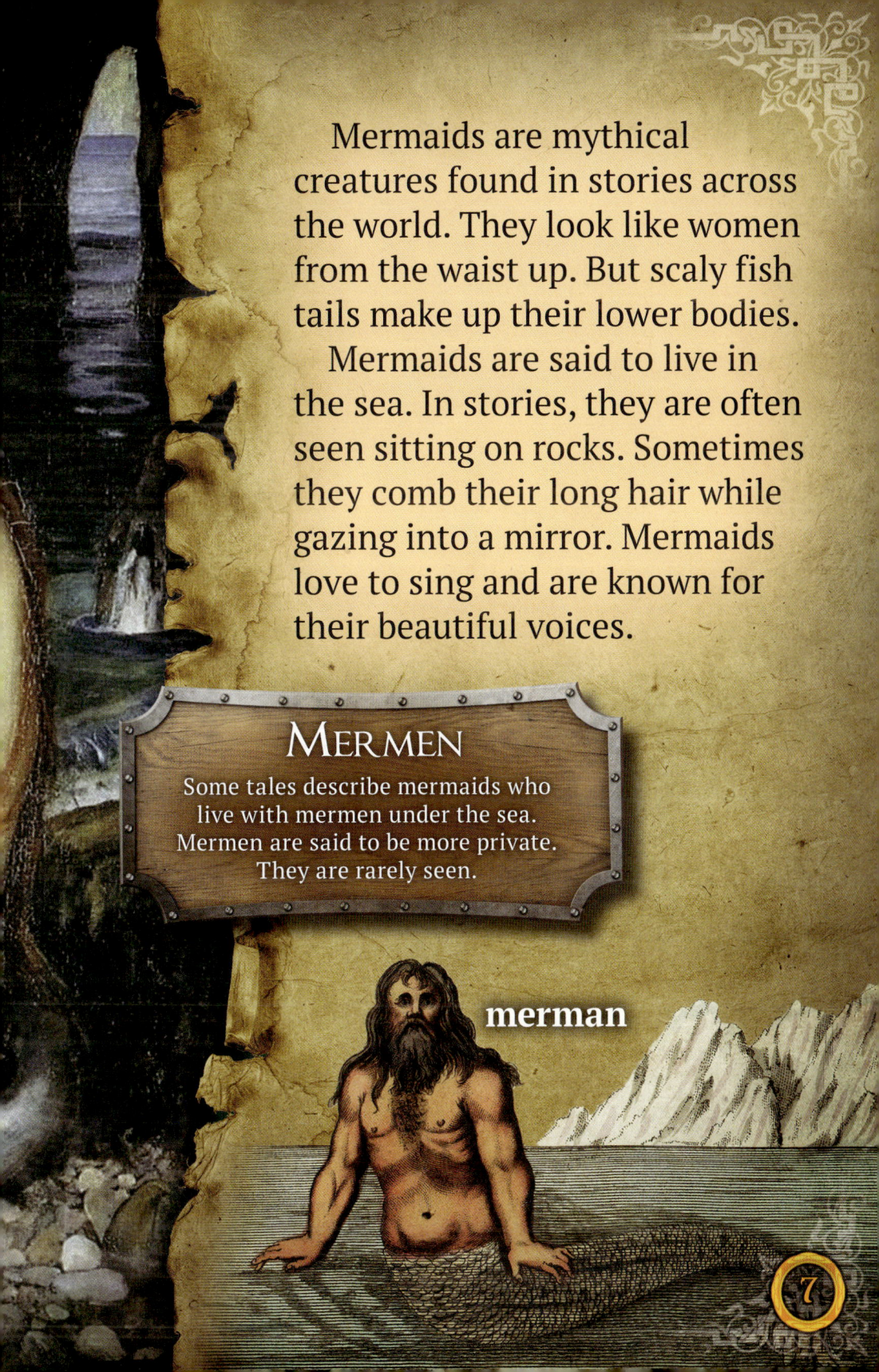

merman

In some **myths**, mermaids are kind to humans. They may even fall in love. But most often, mermaids are bad **omens**.

They sing or call to passing ships. Sailors are **entranced** by their voices and beauty. But it is a trap! Ships sink trying to reach them. Mermaids can also cause storms or floods. Like the sea, they are beautiful but dangerous.

WATER GODS, SIRENS, AND SIGHTINGS

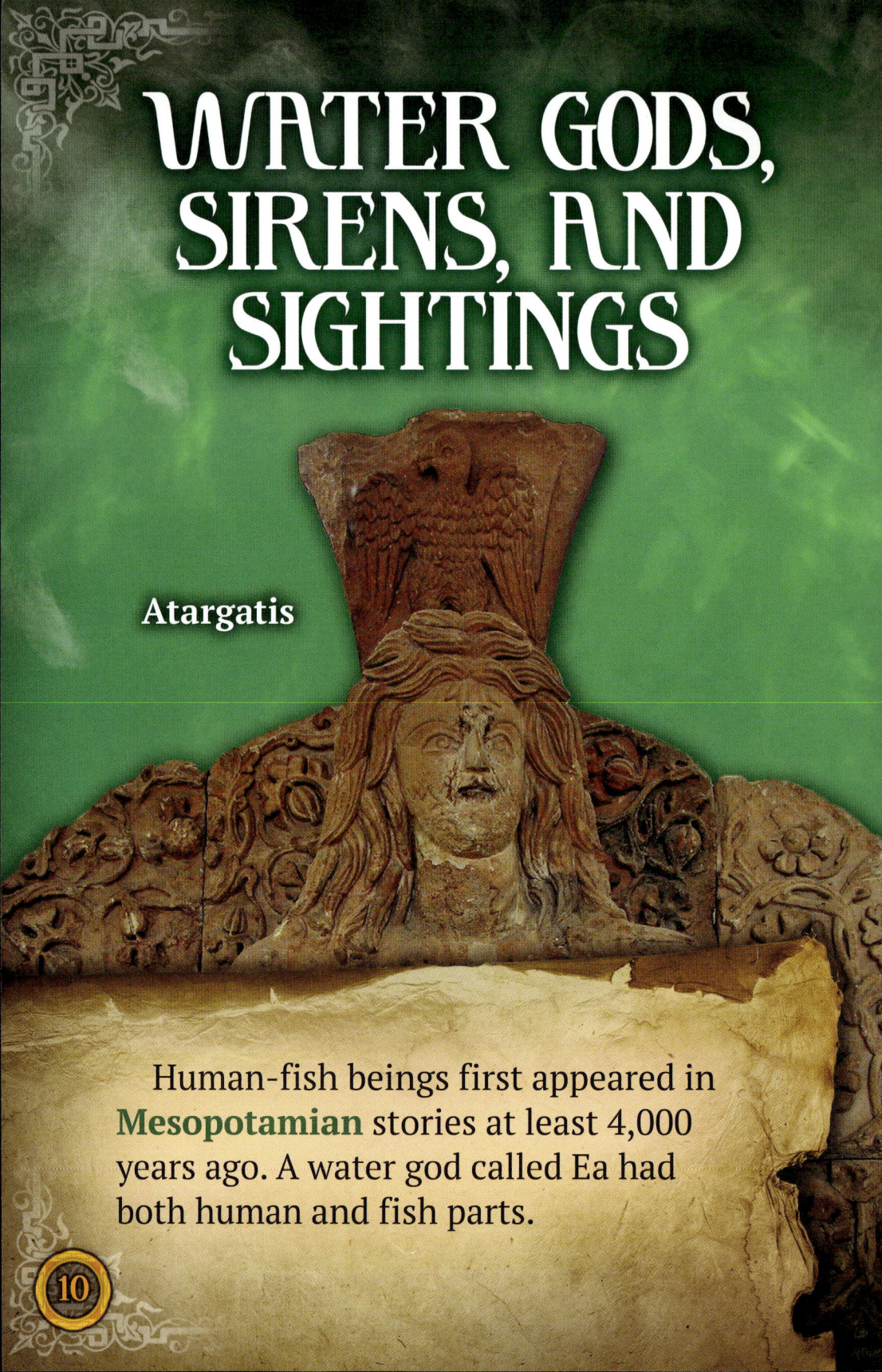

Atargatis

Human-fish beings first appeared in **Mesopotamian** stories at least 4,000 years ago. A water god called Ea had both human and fish parts.

Later, the Syrian goddess Atargatis is said to have jumped or fallen into a lake. She turned into a fish with a woman's head.

Mermaid Origin

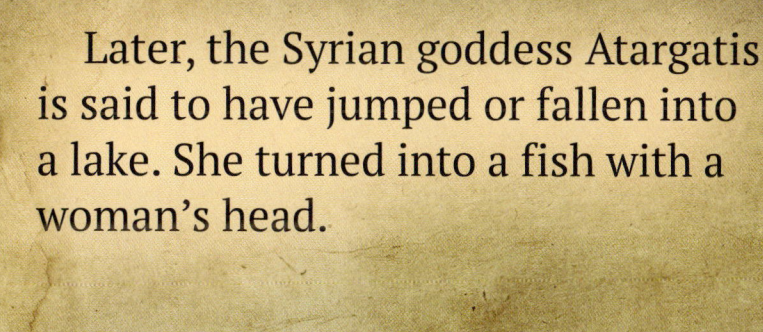

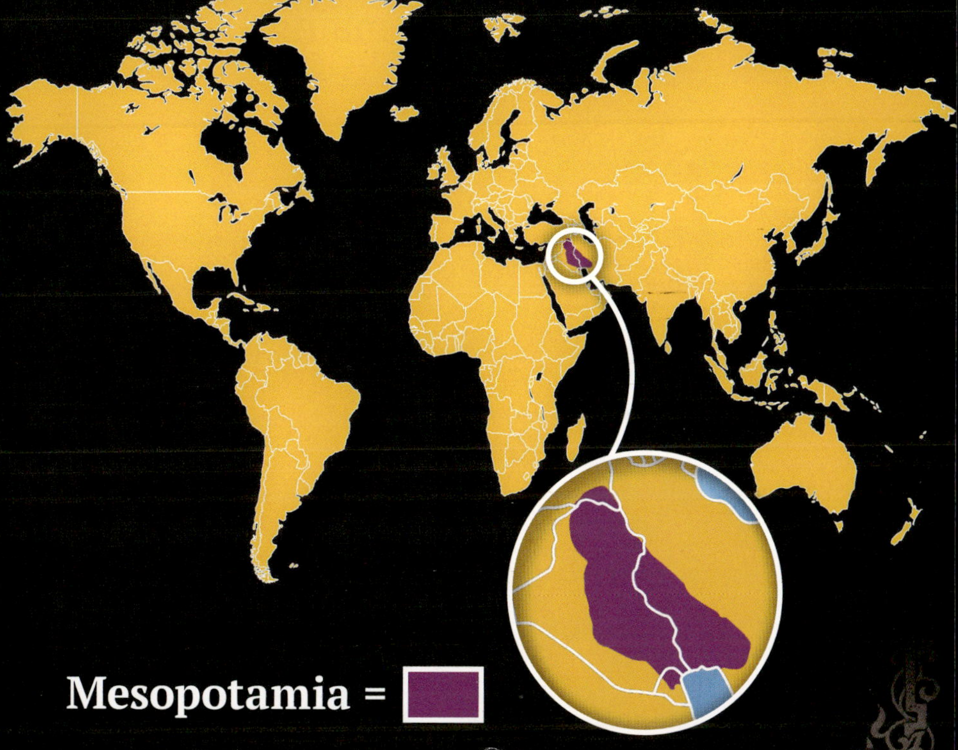

Mesopotamia =

Creatures in ancient Greek myths **inspired** many modern mermaid stories. The Greek sea god Triton had a fish tail.

Early **literature** introduced **sirens**. In Homer's *Odyssey*, they haunted the seas. Their singing lured sailors to their doom. Sirens in early art were shown as bird women. But by the **Middle Ages**, they were almost always described as mermaids.

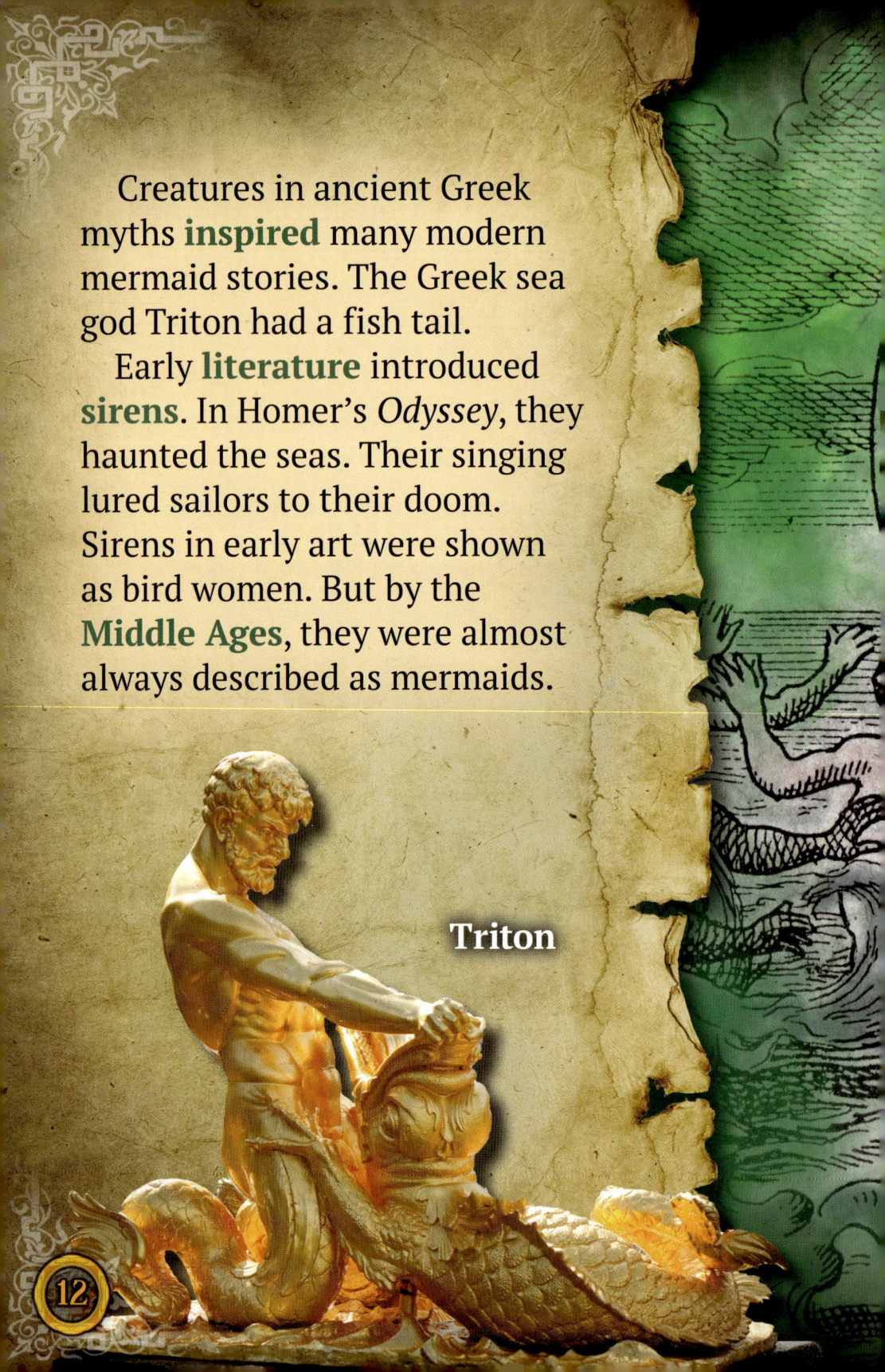

Triton

illustration of Homer's *Odyssey*

sirens

In the Middle Ages, many believed each land creature had its match in the sea. People thought mermaids must be real! Sailors often reported seeing them.

During his 1493 **voyage**, Christopher Columbus believed he spotted three mermaids. In 1608, a sailor described seeing a mermaid with long, black hair and a speckled tail. Similar reports are sometimes made today!

The Feejee Mermaid

In 1842, showman P.T. Barnum claimed to have the body of a real mermaid on display. Many believed it was real. But it turned out to be fake.

Mermaid Timeline

2000s BCE: Human-fish sea gods appear in Mesopotamian mythology

700 BCE: Homer's *Odyssey* mentions sirens

1493: Christopher Columbus claims to spot mermaids

Experts agree that mermaids are not real. They think dugongs, manatees, or seals inspired mermaid myths and sightings. These animals have mermaid-like tails. They often surface to breathe.

Seals warm themselves on rocks. From far away, these **mammals** can look human. Some note that tired sailors might **hallucinate** mermaids.

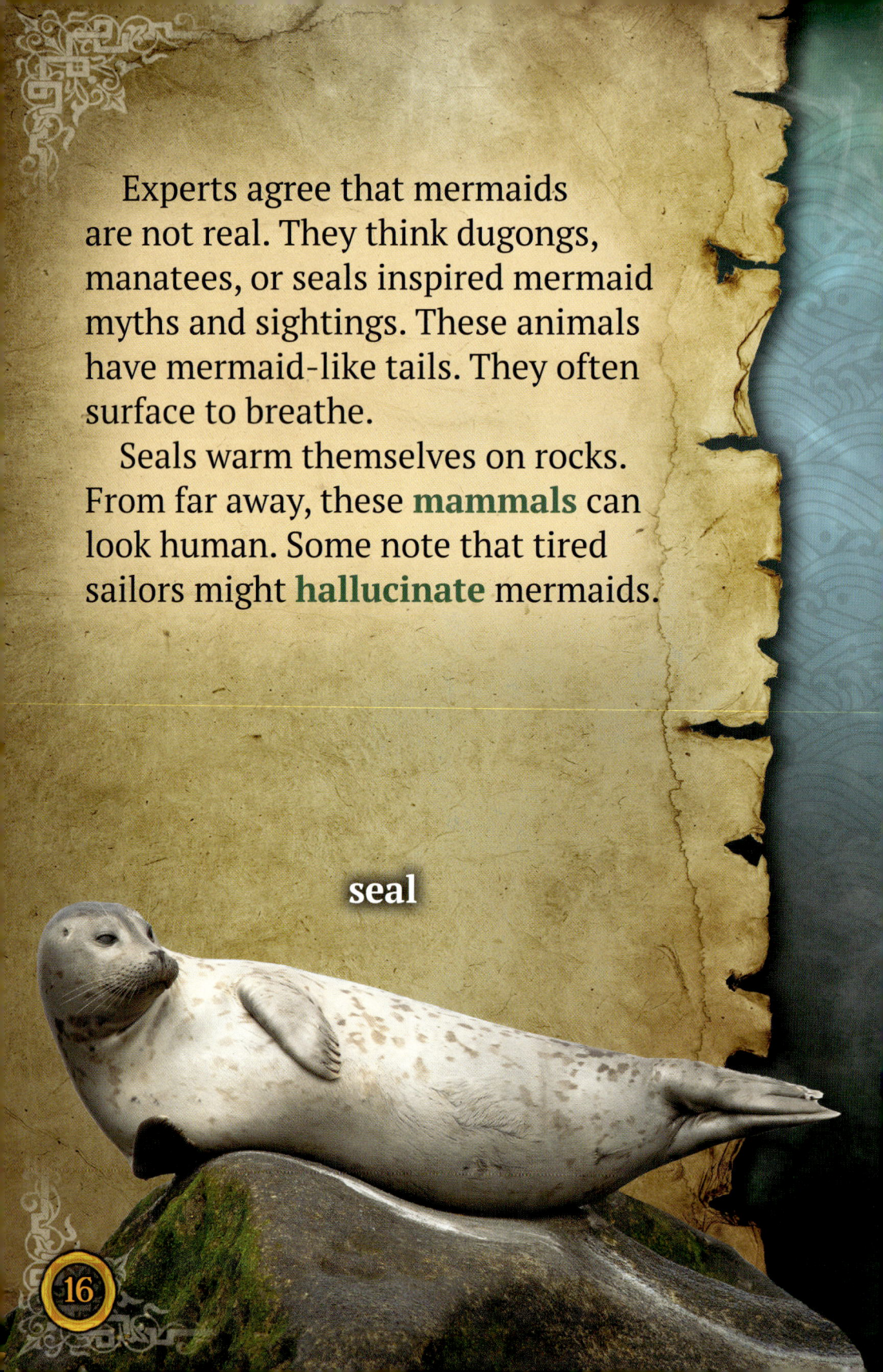

seal

Mermaid Myths Around the World

**merrow
(Ireland)**

**selkie
(Scotland)**

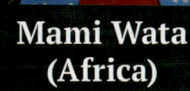
**Mami Wata
(Africa)**

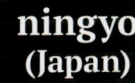
**ningyo
(Japan)**

17

THE NOT-SO-SCARY MERMAID

Modern science has uncovered many mysteries of the sea. Mermaid stories have become less scary. Mermaids in today's stories are more likely to befriend humans. Disney's 1989 movie *The Little Mermaid* is a famous example. In the 2019 video game *The Legend of Zelda: Link's Awakening*, Link finds a mermaid's lost necklace. In return, she gives him an item he needs for his quest.

Mermaids and Marriage

In some stories, a man steals an object from a mermaid. This traps her in human form so he can marry her. In others, mermaids bring men underwater. It is not clear if the men can survive.

Media Mention

Fairy Tale: The Little Mermaid

Written By: Hans Christian Andersen

Year Released: 1837

Summary: A mermaid falls in love with a prince, trades her voice for painful legs, does not marry the prince, and turns into sea foam

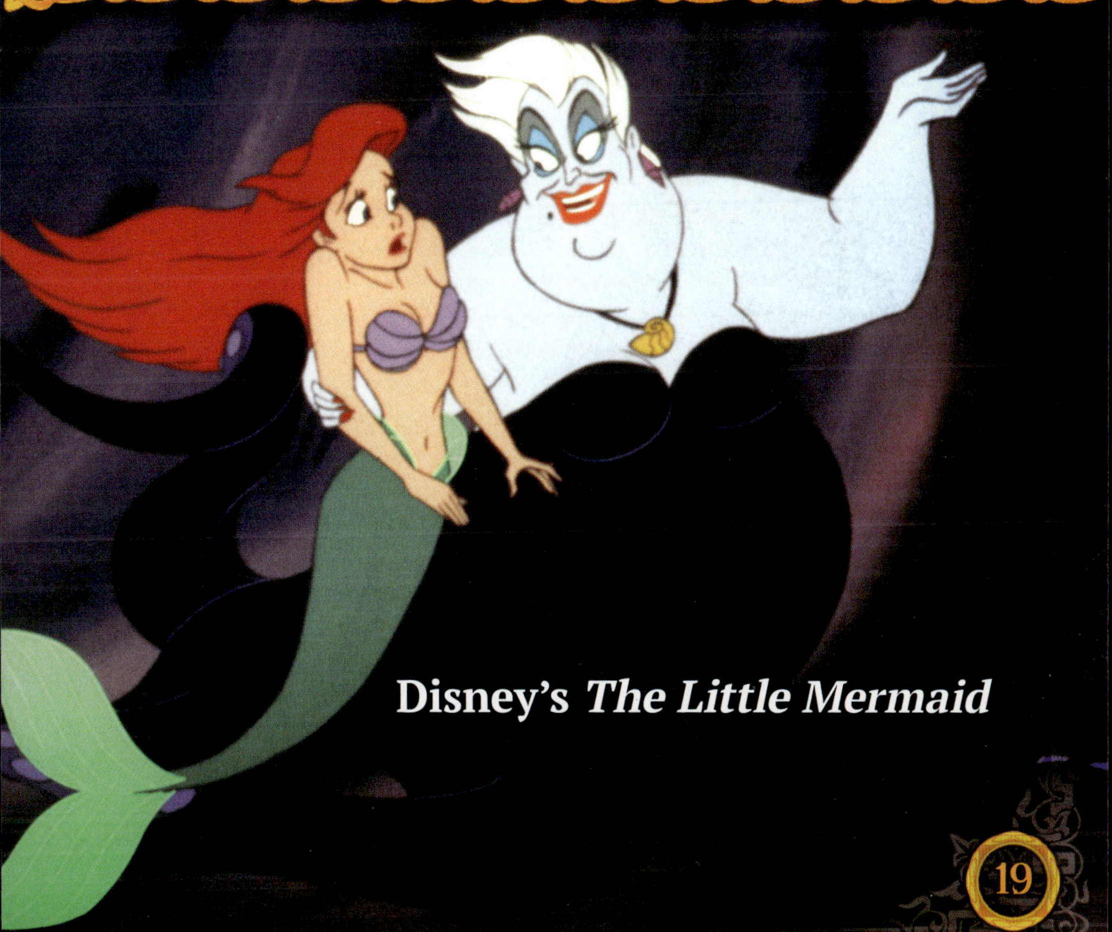

Disney's *The Little Mermaid*

Most people no longer believe in mermaids. Instead, they think of them as friendly and playful characters. Many enjoy dressing up as mermaids. Some swim with **monofins** or train for underwater shows.

People love to imagine magical underwater worlds. Mermaids are classic **symbols** of the danger, mystery, and beauty of the sea!

monofin

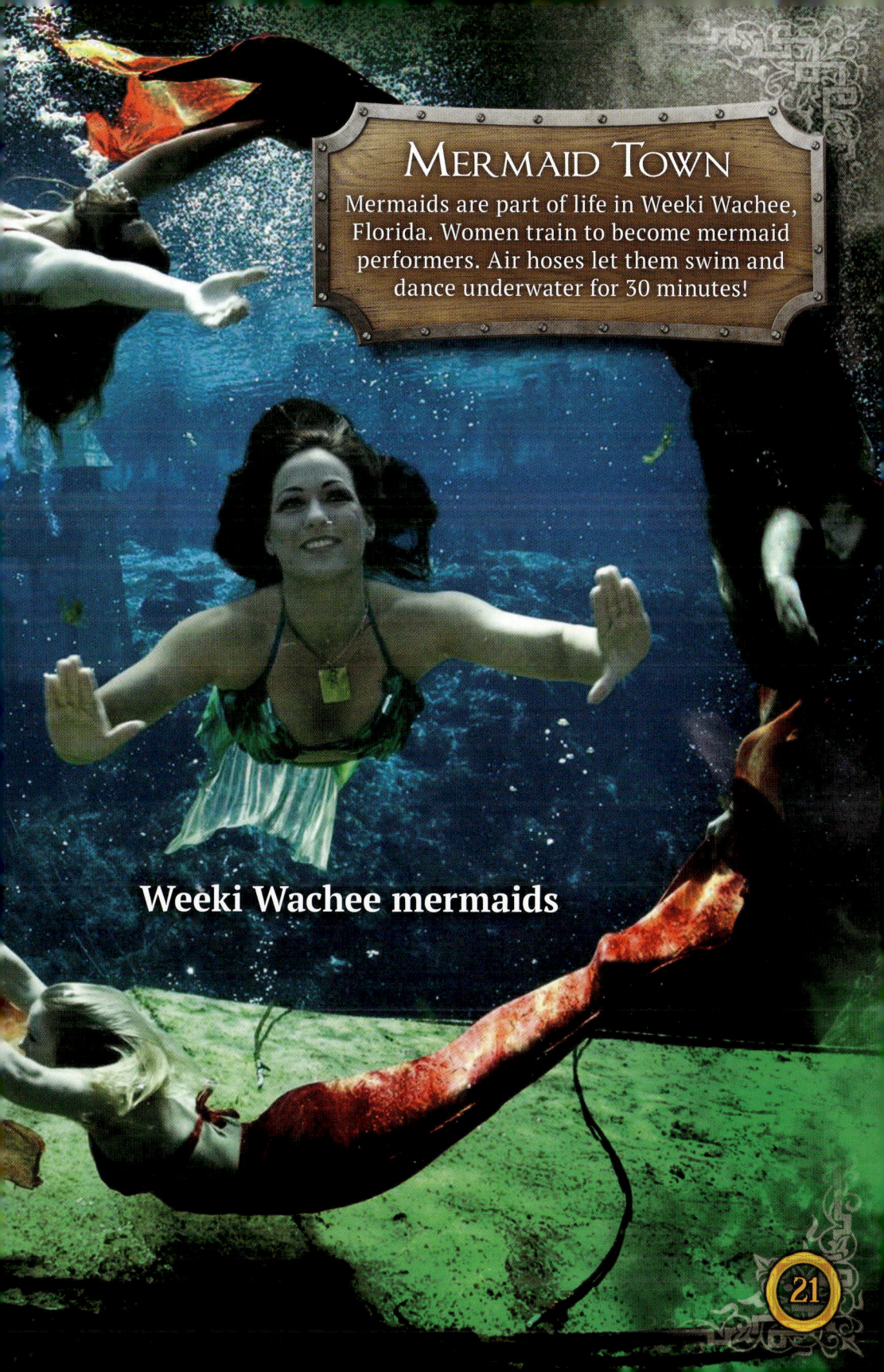

Mermaid Town

Mermaids are part of life in Weeki Wachee, Florida. Women train to become mermaid performers. Air hoses let them swim and dance underwater for 30 minutes!

Weeki Wachee mermaids

GLOSSARY

entranced—filled with wonder and delight

hallucinate—to see or hear something that is not really there

inspired—gave someone an idea about what to do or create

literature—written works, often books, that are highly respected

mammals—warm-blooded animals that have backbones and feed their young milk

Mesopotamian—related to a region of southwestern Asia where many ancient civilizations began

Middle Ages—the period of European history from about 500 to 1500 CE

monofins—fins used in underwater sports or activities that attach to the swimmer's feet; monofins allow users to swim like mermaids.

myths—ancient stories about the beliefs or history of a group of people; myths also try to explain events.

omens—signs or warnings about future events

sirens—part-human beings from Greek mythology whose singing lured sailors to their deaths

symbols—things that stand for something else

voyage—a long journey by sea

TO LEARN MORE

AT THE LIBRARY

Meister, Cari. *Mermaids*. North Mankato, Minn.: Capstone, 2020.

O'Brien, Cynthia. *Mermaid Myths*. New York, N.Y.: Gareth Stevens Publishing, 2018.

Widrig, Taylor. *The Mermaid Handbook*. Toronto, Ont.: Nimbus Publishing, 2020.

ON THE WEB

FACTSURFER

Factsurfer.com gives you a safe, fun way to find more information.

1. Go to www.factsurfer.com

2. Enter "mermaids" into the search box and click 🔍.

3. Select your book cover to see a list of related content.

INDEX

appearance, 7, 10, 11, 12, 14

around the world, 17

art, 12

Atargatis, 10, 11

Barnum, P.T., 14

Columbus, Christopher, 14

Ea, 10

explanations, 16

fish, 5, 7, 10, 11, 12

history, 10, 11, 12, 14, 18

humans, 8, 10, 16, 18

Legend of Zelda, The: Link's Awakening, 18

literature, 12

Little Mermaid, The (fairy tale), 19

Little Mermaid, The (movie), 18, 19

mermen, 7

Mesopotamia, 10, 11

Middle Ages, 12, 14

monofins, 20

myths, 8, 12, 16, 17

Odyssey, 12, 13

omens, 8

origin, 11

powers, 9

sailors, 4, 5, 9, 12, 14, 16

sea, 4, 5, 7, 12, 14, 18, 20

sirens, 12, 13

song, 4, 7, 9, 12

symbols, 20

timeline, 14-15

Triton, 12

Weeki Wachee, Florida, 21

The images in this book are reproduced through the courtesy of: Ironika, front cover (hero), p. 3; Lana Kray, front cover (background); Niday Picture Library/ Alamy, p. 4; katalinks, pp. 4-5; Artepics/ Alamy, pp. 6-7; Florilegius/ Alamy, p. 7; The Print Collection/ Alamy, pp. 8-9; Lala love/ Wiki Commons, pp. 10-11; Bogomayako/ Alamy, p. 12; SPCollection/ Alamy, pp. 12-13; Daderot/ Wiki Commons, p. 14; The History Collection/ Alamy, p. 15 (top); InterFoto/ Alamy, pp. 15 (middle), 17 (bottom); Lanmas/ Alamy, p. 15 (bottom); Dancestrokes, p. 16; Jef Thompson, p. 17 (top left); Andreas F. Borchert/ Wiki Commons, p. 17 (top middle); Pictures From History/ Newscom, p. 17 (top right); Allstar Picture Library/ Alamy, pp. 18-19; Hilary Morgan/ Alamy, p. 19 (top); Elina Manninen, p. 20; mavrixphoto/ Newscom, pp. 20-21; Mayer George, p. 23; Michel Seelen, pp. 22-23 (background), 24 (background).